Counting Books

Baby Animals 1, 2, 3

A Counting Book of Animal Offspring

by Barbara Knox

Reading Consultant:
Jennifer Norford, consultant
Mid-continent Research for Education and Learning

Capstone press
Mankato, Minnesota

A+ Books are published by Capstone Press
P.O. Box 669, 151 Good Counsel Drive, Mankato, Minnesota 56002
http://www.capstone-press.com

1 2 3 4 5 6 08 07 06 05 04 03

Library of Congress Cataloging-in-Publication Data
Knox, Barbara.
    Baby animals 1,2,3: a counting book of animal offspring / by Barbara Knox.
    p. cm.—(Counting books)
    Summary: Simple text describes the activities of baby animals, from one puppy to ten kittens.
    Includes bibliographical references and index.
    ISBN 0-7368-1675-5 (hardcover)
    1. Counting—Juvenile literature. 2. Animals—Infancy—Juvenile literature. [1. Animals—Infancy.
2. Counting.] I. Title: Baby animals 123. II. Title: Baby Animals one, two, three. III. Title. IV. Series.
QA113 .K625 2003
513.2'11—dc21   2002151502

Credits
Sarah L. Schuette, editor; Heather Kindseth, designer; Deirdre Barton, photo researcher
Photo Credits
Bruce Coleman Inc., ducklings in water
Corbis, bears, penguins, single pig
Julie Habel/Corbis, pigs in a basket
Digital Vision, kittens
Mitsuaki Iwago/Minden Pictures, lamb
PhotoDisc, Inc., chicks, ducklings, leopards, puppy

Note to Parents, Teachers, and Librarians
Baby Animals 1,2,3 uses color photographs and a nonfiction format to introduce
children to a variety of baby animals while building mastery of basic counting
skills. It is designed to be read aloud to a pre-reader or to be read independently
by an early reader. The images help early readers and listeners understand the text
and concepts discussed. The book encourages further learning by including the
following sections: Words to Know, Read More, Internet Sites, and Index. Early
readers may need assistance using these features.

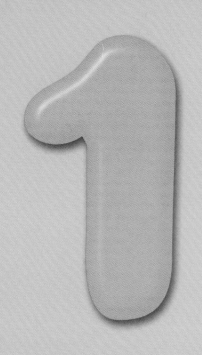

One sad and lonesome puppy waits for a playmate. A young puppy needs to exercise and play.

2

Two leopard cubs wait for their mother. Cubs sometimes stay with their mothers for nearly two years.

Three lambs stand on wobbly legs. Lambs live in a flock with their mother.

9

4

Four bunnies have long, pointy ears. Bunnies can move their ears to hear sounds better.

Five bear cubs have fur to stay warm. In the winter, bears go to sleep. They wake in the spring.

6

Six piglets don't quite fit in a barrel. A group of pigs is called a herd or a drove.

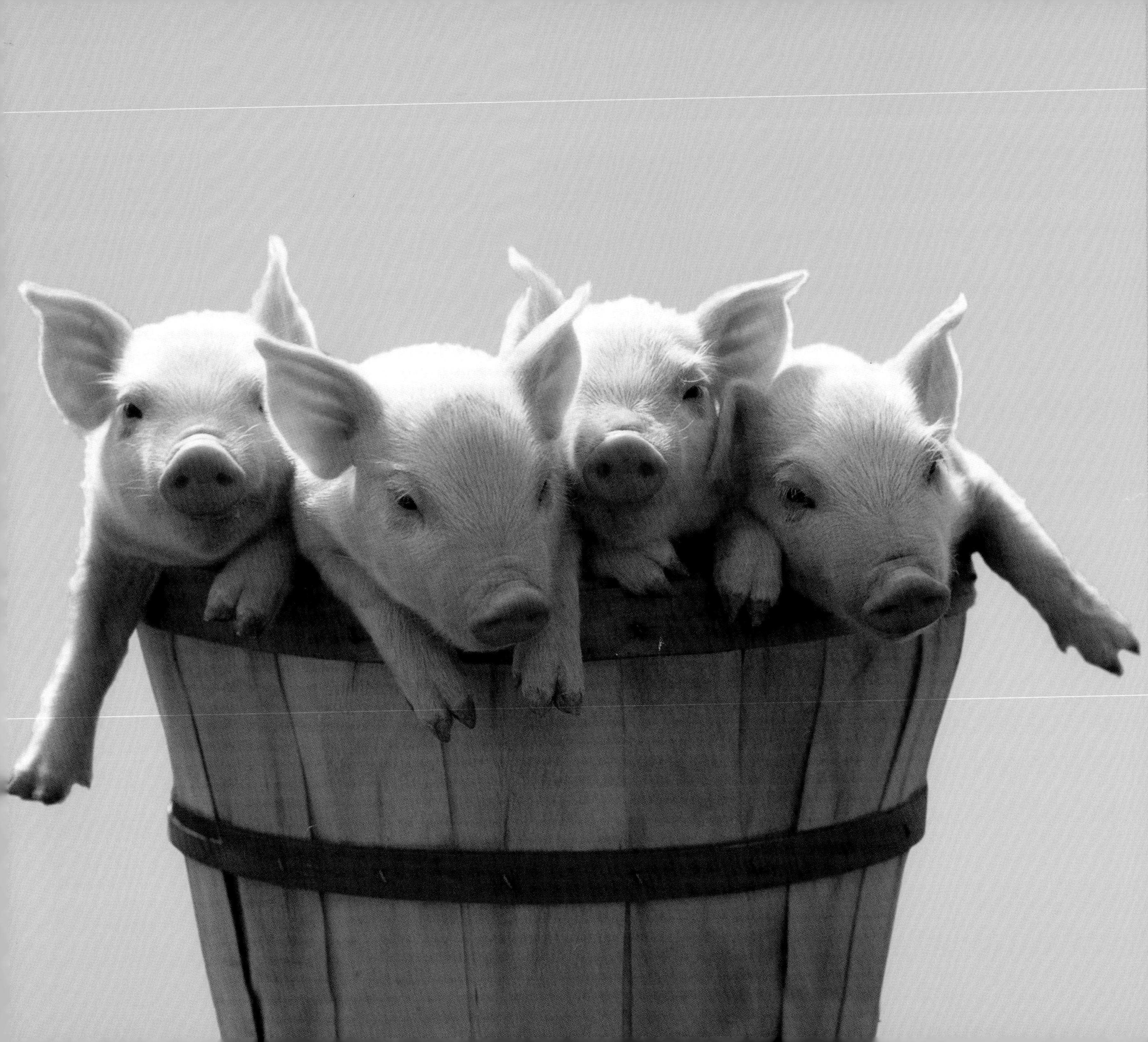

1
2
3
4
5
6
7
8
9
10

7

Seven chicks hatched from seven eggs. It takes about 21 days for a chick egg to hatch.

Eight penguin chicks huddle together. Chicks stay in a group while adult penguins search for food.

9

Nine ducklings sit on webbed feet. They paddle their feet when they swim.

10

Ten kittens pounce and play. Most of their awake time is spent running, jumping, and climbing.

How Many?

Bunnies

Chicks

Penguin chicks

Piglets

Animal Offspring Facts

Dog

- born in litters of three to six puppies
- newborn puppies cannot see or hear
- barks when excited

Rabbit

- bunnies born with eyes closed
- female is a doe; male is a buck
- has good sense of smell

Leopard

- cubs born in a den
- likes to swim
- eats birds, mice, and other animals

Bear

- cubs born in dens
- female is a sow; male is a boar
- uses sharp claws to catch food

Sheep

- female is a ewe; male is a ram
- a ewe usually has two lambs
- has hooves for feet

Pig

- born in litters of nine to ten piglets
- female is a sow; male is a boar
- rolls in mud to keep cool

Chicken

- hatches after 21 days
- female is a hen; male is a rooster
- has wings, but cannot fly very far

Duck

- uses long bill to peck at food
- grows up quickly
- lives near water

Penguin

- both parents take care of eggs
- group of chicks is a creche
- makes many calls or sounds

Cat

- born in litters of four to six kittens
- sees and hears after two weeks
- has a rough tongue

Words to Know

barrel (BA-ruhl)—a large container with curved sides

exercise (EK-sur-size)—physical activity that helps keep animals and people healthy

flock (FLOK)—a group of the same kind of animal that lives, travels, or eats together

hatch (HACH)—to break out of an egg; some baby animals hatch quickly; others take a long time to hatch.

huddle (HUHD-uhl)—to crowd together in a tight group; some animals huddle together to keep each other warm.

pounce (POUNSS)—to jump on something suddenly and grab hold of it; some animals pounce on their prey.

Read More

Cappetta, Cynthia. *Counting Animals.* Flip & Slide. Norwalk, Conn.: Innovative Kids, 2001.

McGinty, Alice B. *Ten Little Lambs.* New York: Dial Books for Young Readers, 2002.

Van Fleet, Matthew. *Tails.* San Diego, Calif.: Silver Whistle, 2003.

Walton, Rick. *One More Bunny: Adding from One to Ten.* New York: Lothrop, Lee, & Shepard Books, 2000.

Internet Sites

Track down many sites about baby animals. Visit the FACT HOUND at *http://www.facthound.com*

IT IS EASY! IT IS FUN!
1) Go to *http://www.facthound.com*
2) Type in: 0736816755
3) Click on "FETCH IT" and FACT HOUND will find several links hand-picked by our editors.

Relax and let our pal FACT HOUND do the research for you!

Index